THE SECRET OF THE HiDDEN SCROLLS

BOOK FOUR
JOURNEY TO JERICHO

BY M. J. THOMAS

WORTHY kids™

*For the Amazing Kids Editing Team and students
at PCA. Thank you for your help and great ideas.*

—M.J.T.

ISBN: 978-0-8249-5692-9

WorthyKids
Hachette Book Group
1290 Avenue of the Americas
New York, NY 10104

Library of Congress Cataloging-in-Publication Data
Names: Thomas, M. J., 1969- author. | Reed, Lisa (Illustrator) illustrator.
Title: Journey to Jericho / by M. J. Thomas ; interior illustrations by Lisa
    S. Reed.
Description: Nashville, Tennessee : WorthyKids/Ideals, [2018] | Series:
    Secret of the hidden scrolls ; book 4 | Summary: Peter, nine, Mary, ten,
    and their dog, Hank, journey into biblical history to the time of the
    battle of Jericho, where they meet Israelite spies.
Identifiers: LCCN 2018021991 | ISBN 9780824956929 (pbk. : alk. paper)
Subjects: | CYAC: Time travel—Fiction. | Spies— Fiction. | Rahab (Biblical
    figure)—Fiction. | Joshua (Biblical figure)—Fiction. | Jews—History—To
    1200 B.C.—Fiction. | Brothers and sisters—Fiction. | Dogs—Fiction. |
    Jericho—History—Siege, ca. 1400 B.C.—Fiction.
Classification: LCC PZ7.1.T4654 Jou 2018 | DDC [Fic]—dc23 LC record available at https://
lccn.loc.gov/2018021991

Cover illustration by Graham Howells
Interior illustrations by Lisa S. Reed
Designed by Georgina Chidlow-Irvin

Lexile® level 560L

Printed and bound in the U.S.A.
CW
10 9 8 7 6

CONTENTS

PROLOGUE

Nine-year-old Peter and his ten-year-old sister, Mary, stood at the door to the huge, old house and waved as their parents drove away. Peter and Mary and their dog, Hank, would be spending the month with Great-Uncle Solomon.

Peter thought it would be the most boring month ever—until he realized Great-Uncle Solomon was an archaeologist. Great-Uncle Solomon showed them artifacts and treasures and told them stories about his travels around the globe. And then he shared his most amazing discovery of all—the Legend of the Hidden Scrolls! These weren't just

1

dusty old scrolls. They held secrets—and they would lead to travel through time.

Soon Peter, Mary, and Hank were flung back in time to important moments in the Bible. They witnessed the Creation of the earth. They helped Noah load the animals before the flood. They endured the plagues in Egypt. They saw amazing things and had exciting adventures, all while trying to solve the secrets of the scrolls.

Now Peter and Mary are ready for their next adventure . . . as soon as they hear the lion's roar.

The Legend of the Hidden Scrolls

THE SCROLLS CONTAIN THE TRUTH YOU SEEK.
BREAK THE SEAL. UNROLL THE SCROLL.
AND YOU WILL SEE THE PAST UNFOLD.
AMAZING ADVENTURES ARE IN STORE
FOR THOSE WHO FOLLOW THE LION'S ROAR!

THE HIDDEN DOOR

Hank barked and licked Peter's face.

"Okay, okay," said Peter. "I'll get up!"

Peter wiped Hank's slobber off his face and the sleep from his eyes.

Hank jumped off the bed and scratched at the bedroom door.

"Why are you in such a hurry this morning?" asked Peter. He quickly put on his clothes and opened the door.

Hank darted out and trotted down the hallway. Peter followed, running to catch up. Hank slid to a stop in front of Great-Uncle Solomon's library. Peter stopped too and looked up at the large wooden doors. Hank scratched the doors and wagged his tail.

"Did you hear something in the library?" said Peter. He pressed his ear against the door but didn't hear anything. He tried the large handle shaped like a lion's head. "Locked! I guess we have to wait to go on our next adventure."

Hank lowered his head and stopped wagging his tail.

"You know the Legend of the Scrolls." Peter did his best impression of Great-Uncle Solomon.

"The scrolls contain the truth you seek. Break the seal, unroll the scroll, and you will see the past unfold. Amazing adventures are in store for those who follow the lion's roar."

Hank tilted his head as if he understood.

Peter rubbed Hank's head. "We have to wait for the lion's roar." He wondered when they would hear it again. It had been two days since their last adventure back through time to ancient Egypt, and he could hardly wait for the next one.

Grrrr!

Hank's ears perked up, and Peter laughed. "That wasn't the lion," he said. "That was my stomach. It's time for breakfast."

Peter stopped by Mary's room to wake her up. He knocked, but she didn't answer. So he opened the door and peeked in. She wasn't there.

"That's strange," said Peter. "Maybe she already went to breakfast."

Peter and Hank headed down the long hallway to the kitchen, but Mary wasn't there. Neither was Great-Uncle Solomon. That was weird, because he was in the kitchen every morning drinking coffee and reading his Bible.

"Where is everybody?" Peter wondered aloud.

Hank's ears perked up again, and he tilted his head.

"Did you hear something?" said Peter.

He followed Hank into the living room, but no one was there except the shiny suit of armor across the room. Peter felt like it was watching him. He moved back and forth in front of the armor, but it didn't move. He knew the armor wasn't alive, but sometimes he just wasn't sure. The house felt a little eerie when he was alone.

A noise came from the second floor. Peter and Hank scurried up the stairs in time to see Mary going into a room.

"Let's scare Mary," said Peter.

Peter snuck into the room with Hank right behind him. Mary was looking at some old pottery. Peter grabbed her shoulder.

Mary spun around in a karate stance.

Peter jumped back. Hank scrambled toward the door, but Peter bumped into a shelf full of pottery jars and bowls. The shelf shifted, and the pottery wobbled. One jar fell off. Peter dove and caught it before it smashed on the floor. It had a red and black zig-zag design on it.

Mary put her hands on her hips. "Why were you spying on me?"

"I wasn't spying on you." Peter carefully put the jar back. "I was just trying to find you and Great-Uncle Solomon."

"I was trying to find him too," said Mary.

Peter went to the door and shouted for Great-Uncle Solomon.

"Shhh," said Mary. "Let's straighten this shelf and pottery before he finds us."

As they were scooting the shelf back, Peter saw a large tapestry covering the wall behind the shelf. It was blue, red, and purple with angels stitched on it in gold thread.

"That's fancy," said Peter.

"I wonder why it's hidden behind a shelf," said Mary.

They scooted the shelf forward. Hank scratched at the tapestry.

Peter shoved the tapestry to the side, and his mouth dropped open. He had uncovered a secret door. "Look at this!"

Mary leaned in. "Wow!" She put her hand on her chin. "I wonder what Great-Uncle Solomon is hiding?"

"Let's find out." Peter turned the doorknob.

"Wait!" said Mary. She twisted her hair like she

always did when she was nervous. "Maybe we're not supposed to go in there."

Hank sniffed along the bottom of the door.

"Come on, Mary," said Peter. "I know you like secrets." He dashed to the door of the room and looked down the hallway. "The coast is clear."

"Okay." Mary nodded. "But let's hurry."

Peter ran back to the secret door, opened it, and peeked in. The room was filled with old gadgets. Across the room in a corner, there was a desk with a black briefcase on it.

"I wonder what's in the briefcase," said Peter, heading for the desk.

Hank whined.

"Look out!" said Mary. "There's a—"

Peter felt his toe snag on something, and he fell forward.

"A wire," said Mary, as an alarm went off.

She ran for the door. "Let's get out of here!"

Hank nudged Peter, and they started after Mary.

But there was Great-Uncle Solomon, standing at the door to the secret room.

Peter, Hank, and Mary froze in their tracks.

"Looking for something?" asked Great-Uncle Solomon.

"We were looking for you," said Peter.

Great-Uncle Solomon adjusted his round glasses. "Seems like a strange place to look."

"Peter made me do it," said Mary. "I told him we shouldn't come in here."

Peter scowled. "Thanks."

"*Ruff!*" barked Hank.

"Are you going to turn on me too?" said Peter.

Great-Uncle Solomon petted Hank's head. "It's okay," he said. "You can go anywhere in the house you want. My house is your house."

Peter wiped the sweat off his forehead and nodded to Mary. "I told you it was all right. You should trust me."

"Right," said Mary. She looked up at Great-Uncle Solomon. "Why do you have a secret room and all these old gadgets?"

"I wasn't always an archaeologist," said Great-Uncle Solomon. He looked around as if he wanted to make sure no one else was listening. Then he said, "I used to be a spy."

CODE NAME: THE OWL

"You don't look like a spy," said Mary.

Great-Uncle Solomon walked across the room and put on a black jacket. "How about now?"

Mary tilted her head. "Yeah, I guess you look a little like a spy."

He took off his round glasses, then grabbed a black hat and sunglasses from the desk and slipped them on.

"Yes," said Peter. "Now you look like a spy."

"How did you become a spy?" asked Mary.

"It was many, many years ago." Great-Uncle

Solomon took off his sunglasses and put his round glasses back on. "I was an archeology student at the university, and the war had been going on for several years. One day I received a top-secret letter in my mailbox."

"What did it say?" asked Mary.

Great-Uncle Solomon opened the black briefcase, pulled out the old letter, and handed it to Mary.

She opened it and read, "We have been watching you, and we think you should be part of the ISA. Meet me at the library in the History section at 11:11. Don't be late and come alone. Sincerely, S. G. Morley."

"What is the ISA?" said Peter.

Mary rolled her eyes. "It's the International Spy Agency," she said, like everyone should know.

"Did you go?" asked Peter.

"Yes," said Great-Uncle Solomon. "And I became a spy."

Hank had been sniffing around the room. He brought Great-Uncle Solomon a walkie-talkie.

Peter found the other walkie-talkie, pushed the red button, and spoke into it. *Chhhh.* "What was it like being a spy?"

Great-Uncle Solomon pushed the button on his walkie-talkie and answered. *Chhhh.* "It was exciting, but sometimes it was very dangerous. Everyone was trying to catch me." Then he handed the walkie-talkie to Mary.

"How do we become spies?" said Mary.

Great-Uncle Solomon reached into the black briefcase and pulled out a book titled *Top Secret Spy Training Manual*. He handed it to Mary. "This will tell you everything you need to know."

Mary opened the book and started reading.

Peter looked over her shoulder and saw a handwritten name on the first page. "Who is The Owl?"

Great-Uncle Solomon laughed, "I haven't heard that name in so long! The Owl was my secret code name."

Peter glanced at Mary. She loved secrets. Her eyes were open wide.

Great-Uncle Solomon explained how secret code names had a long history. "Even God had a secret code name he revealed to the Israelites. God told his secret name to Moses at the burning bush."

"What is it?" asked Mary.

Great-Uncle Solomon grabbed some paper and a pen. "It is the Hebrew letters Y-H-W-H." He wrote the Hebrew letters on the paper. "Some people pronounce it Yahweh."

Mary squinted at the paper. "There's nothing on here!"

Great-Uncle Solomon looked at his pen and laughed. "Oh, yeah. This is one of my spy pens with invisible ink."

"How can we read it?" said Mary.

Great-Uncle Solomon picked up a tiny flashlight. "Shine this on the paper."

When Mary shined the special blue light, Hebrew letters appeared.

"That's so cool!" said Peter. "Can I have it?"

"Of course," said Great-Uncle Solomon.

"Thanks!" Peter examined the flashlight then stuck it in his pocket.

"We need secret code names," said Mary.

"That's true," said Great-Uncle Solomon. "Every spy needs a secret code name."

"Do mine first," said Peter.

Great-Uncle Solomon rubbed his chin as he studied Peter. "Your code name is The Bear, because you are strong and brave."

"What about me?" asked Mary.

"Your code name is The Monkey," said Great-Uncle Solomon, "because you are smart and curious."

"She does like figuring things out," said Peter.

"What else do we need to be spies?" asked Mary.

"You need to dress like spies," said Great-Uncle Solomon.

Peter and Mary ran downstairs to their bedrooms and dressed in black clothes from head to toe. Peter also grabbed his brown leather adventure bag. They ran back to the secret spy room.

Great-Uncle Solomon looked up from searching through drawers in the desk. "Now you look like spies," he said. He handed several gadgets to Peter. "These might be helpful on your next adventure."

Peter put the gadgets and walkie-talkies in his adventure bag. It was too bad Great-Uncle Solomon wasn't a spy anymore. "Why did you stop being a spy and become an archaeologist?"

"Well, many years ago, I was on a secret mission to find art and ancient artifacts stolen from museums by the enemy," said Great-Uncle Solomon. "During the mission, I discovered an artifact that could help prove the Bible is true. From that moment, I dedicated my life to finding more artifacts that prove the Bible is true."

"What did you find?" asked Mary.

Roar!

The lion's roar echoed through the house.

"I promise to tell you when you get back from your adventure," said Great-Uncle Solomon.

Peter, Mary, and Hank ran downstairs and sprinted past the suit of armor. Peter slid to a stop in front of the tall library doors. He turned the lion's-head handle.

Click!

Peter swung the door open, and they ran in.

Roar! The sound came from the tall

bookshelves on the right. Peter tightened his grip on the adventure bag as Mary looked for the red book with the lion's head painted in gold on the cover. She quickly found it. As she pulled it out, the bookshelf slid open to reveal the hidden room. It was dark except for a glowing clay pot that held the scrolls in the center of the room.

Mary ran to the pot and looked through the scrolls. "Let's open this one."

"What's on the red wax seal?" asked Peter.

"It looks like a box with two angels' wings spread across the top," said Mary.

"Let's see where the scroll takes us!" said Peter.

Mary broke the wax seal holding the scroll together.

The walls shook. Books fell to the floor. The library crumbled around them and disappeared. Then everything was quiet.

Trouble in the Tabernacle

Peter reached down and touched sandy ground. "It looks like we're back in the desert," he said. He looked up at a wall with strange patterns on it. "But we're not outside."

Mary nodded. "I think we're in some kind of large tent."

A warm light filled the tent. It flickered against the purple, blue, and red patterns stitched into the walls.

Hank was sniffing around one of the tall golden posts holding up the tent. "Come here, Hank," said Peter. "We'd better be careful in here. This is one fancy tent."

All the light in the tent came from one big candlestick with seven branches and seven flickering flames. Peter walked over to the candlestick. "It's taller than me," he said. He ran his hand over one of the branches. "I think this candlestick is made of pure gold."

Mary peered over Peter's shoulder. "It's a menorah," she said, like Peter should know.

Peter could tell that Mary was about to launch into a history lesson. He looked over at Hank, who had found something more interesting on the other side of the tent: a golden table. "Food!" said Peter.

He ran to the fancy table and counted twelve small loaves of bread on top. His stomach

growled loudly, and he reached for a loaf.

Mary grabbed his hand. "I don't think the bread is for us."

Hank raced across the sand, barking at a gold box with golden horns coming out of the top corners. Peter and Mary ran after him.

Smoke was rising out of the top of the box. "That smells good," said Peter. "It reminds me of one of Mom's candles." Peter missed his mom and dad. It seemed like a long time had passed since they had taken him and Mary to stay at Great-Uncle Solomon's house while they traveled to Africa.

Peter stood a little closer to Mary, who was studying a huge curtain hanging behind the smoldering box. It was blue and purple and red and stretched from the desert floor to the ceiling. The colorful curtain was decorated with large angels stitched with gold thread.

"I wonder what's behind the curtain," said Peter.

"I don't think you should look," said Mary.

Peter ignored her and reached for the curtain.

"*Woof!*" Hank barked.

Peter jumped back.

Glowing smoke slowly rolled out from under the curtain and began to fill the tent.

Peter and Mary backed away. Hank growled and ran to the other end of the tent.

Peter heard voices and turned. "Someone's coming," he said.

"We better hide," whispered Mary.

Peter, Mary, and Hank slid under the golden table. Peter held his breath as he watched a pair of feet walk across the sand.

A big voice spoke from behind the curtain. "MOSES IS DEAD. NOW IT'S TIME FOR YOU TO TAKE THE PEOPLE ACROSS THE JORDAN INTO THE LAND THAT I PROMISED TO GIVE TO ISRAEL."

"That sounds just like the voice we heard during Creation," whispered Peter.

The big voice boomed through the tent. "EVERYWHERE YOU STEP, I WILL GIVE YOU AND ISRAEL THAT LAND. REMEMBER TO READ AND FOLLOW THE COMMANDMENTS I GAVE TO MOSES. BE STRONG AND COURAGEOUS! DO NOT BE AFRAID FOR I, THE LORD

YOUR GOD, WILL BE WITH YOU WHEREVER YOU GO."

The glowing smoke rolled back under the curtain. Only the warm light of the menorah filled the tent.

Peter sat very still as he watched the feet turn and walk toward the entrance of the tent. His heart pounded.

"*Grrrr.*" Hank growled.

The feet paused, stepped up to the golden table, and stopped. A man bent down and looked into Peter's eyes.

"How did you get into the Tabernacle?" asked the man.

Peter gulped. He turned to Mary. When she didn't respond, he said, "It's hard to explain."

The man grabbed Peter by the arm and pulled him out from under the table.

"Wait!" said Mary.

But the man didn't wait. He tugged Peter out of the Tabernacle. Peter could hear Mary and Hank behind him. They stepped out into the hot desert sun in a courtyard surrounded by white curtains. Several priests who had been standing around a large bronze altar ran to them.

"Joshua," said one of the priests. "Where did you find these intruders?"

"They were in the Tabernacle," said Joshua.

"How did they sneak past us and get in there?" asked another priest.

"Maybe they are spies," said Joshua. "Guards!"

A group of about ten men with shields and swords rushed into the courtyard. They surrounded Peter, Mary, and Hank.

Peter held his bag tightly under his arm and muttered, "This isn't going well."

THE PROMISE

"Guards," said Joshua. "Take these spies away from here."

"Wait," said Peter. "We're not spies."

Joshua walked slowly around them. "I can tell from your strange clothes that you're not from around here," he said. "I know spies when I see them. I used to be one."

"But we're not spies," said Mary.

Joshua rubbed his long gray beard. "You look familiar," he said. "You remind me of some children and a dog that escaped Egypt and crossed the Red Sea with us, but we never saw them again."

Peter's heart pounded in his chest. He didn't say a word.

Joshua shook his head. "But that's impossible. It was forty years ago."

Peter laughed nervously. "That would be hard since I'm only nine years old."

"True," said Joshua. "So where have you come from?"

Mary looked at Peter and said, "We have come on a long journey. We would like to help you if we can."

Joshua looked at Mary and wrinkled his forehead. "How can I be certain you are on my side?" he asked.

Peter wasn't sure where Mary was going with this. "Yes, Mary," he said. "Tell Joshua how he can be sure."

Mary scratched her head and thought. Then she bent down and wrote the Hebrew letters Y-H-W-H in the sand with her finger.

"You know the secret name of God that he revealed to Moses!" Joshua said as he read the letters in the sand. "These children are for us and not against us. Guards, you can leave."

The guards lowered their swords and left.

"Since you are believers in the one true God," said Joshua, "you will be our guests, and we will keep you safe." He scratched Hank's head.

Hank wagged his tail.

"You must be tired from your long journey," said Joshua. "Come with me."

Peter, Mary, and Hank followed Joshua out of the courtyard. Small tents surrounded the Tabernacle as far as Peter could see. Many of the tents had small wooden pens beside them filled with sheep. Hank growled at the sheep as they walked past.

Joshua stopped and pointed to a tent. "Welcome to your new home."

Peter peeked in. It was big enough for all three of them. There were comfortable mats on the ground, and a small desk stood in one corner. "Thank you," said Peter.

"Make yourselves comfortable," said Joshua. "I need to tell the people the good news that God told me." He turned to leave.

"Wait!" said Peter. "Can I ask you a question?"

Joshua turned back. "Of course, what would you like to know?"

"In the Tabernacle," said Peter, "God said

something about land that he was giving to Israel." The adventure bag started shaking. Peter held it tight. "What was God talking about?" The bag shook again.

"Many years ago, God promised to give the Israelites a new home," said Joshua. "A beautiful place to raise our families with lots of food and places to play."

"That sounds amazing!" said Mary.

Joshua let out a big sigh. "But we have been wandering around and waiting for a long time to enter the Promised Land."

"How long?" said Mary.

Joshua looked into the sky and thought. "We have waited for over four hundred years."

"Wow!" said Peter. "That *is* a long time."

"Where is the land?" asked Mary.

Joshua pointed west. "See that river?"

Peter squinted. "Yes."

"That's the Jordan River," said Joshua. "The land God promised us is right on the other side."

"That's not very far," said Peter. "Let's go!"

Joshua held up his arm. "Wait," he said. "We have one big problem!"

"What?" said Peter.

"We have to get past Jericho!" Joshua pointed beyond the river to a big city surrounded by tall walls on top of a hill.

Peter thought it looked like one of the mighty fortresses he had seen in a book about knights and kingdoms. "That is a big problem!"

"What can you do?" asked Mary.

"I will wait for God to give me a plan," said Joshua. "But for now, I must tell the people the good news!"

Joshua ducked into a tent and came back out carrying a long, curly horn covered in gold. He held the horn to his lips and blew.

Peter held his ears. "That is one loud trumpet!"

"It's not a trumpet," said Mary. "It's made of a ram's horn, and it's called a *shofar*."

"Is that because you can hear it from show-far away?" Peter said with a grin.

Mary didn't laugh. She never laughed at his jokes.

All the Israelites came out of their tents and gathered to hear what Joshua had to say.

"The time has come!" shouted Joshua. "God is going to lead us into our new home—the Promised Land."

The people cheered, and the sun began to set.

"Let's go back to our tent," said Peter. "The scroll has been shaking. We can figure out the first word."

Inside the tent, Peter put the bag on the little desk and pulled out the scroll. A strong wind blew through the tent. Then it got very quiet, and the hair on Peter's neck stood up. Someone was watching them.

Hank ran to the entrance and growled.

"Someone must be coming," said Mary. "Hide the scroll!"

SNEAKY SUSPECTS

"Hurry, Peter," said Mary. "We can't let anyone see the scroll!"

Peter shoved the scroll back into the bag. Another gust of wind blew the tent flap open.

Peter backed up and hid the bag behind his back.

Michael the angel flew in.

"You scared us!" said Mary. "But I'm glad you're here."

"Where have you been?" asked Peter. "We were almost captured for being spies."

"Are you talking about when Joshua found you in the Tabernacle?" said Michael.

"How did you know we were there?" asked Mary.

"Remember," said Michael, "it's my job to protect you."

"So why didn't you help?" asked Mary.

"It looked like you had it under control," said Michael. "I would have helped if you had needed it."

"That's good to know," said Peter.

"Now, let's go over the rules of your adventure." Michael held up one finger. "First rule: you have to solve the secret of the scroll in fourteen days or you will be stuck here."

Peter pulled the scroll out of the bag. It was shaking in his hand.

"Don't open it yet," said Michael. "I need to finish the rules."

Peter held the scroll close. It had stopped shaking, and he was itching to unroll it.

Michael held up two fingers. "Second rule: you can't tell anyone where you are from or that you came from the future."

Peter and Mary nodded their heads.

Michael held up three fingers. "Third rule: you can't try to change the past. Okay, now you can open the scroll."

Peter unrolled it. "It looks like it's five words written in Hebrew."

Mary looked over Peter's shoulder. "Isn't that the Hebrew word for God?"

The first word glowed and transformed into the word GOD.

"You're off to a good start," said Michael. "Remember to be on guard for the enemy, Satan. He doesn't want the Israelites to enter the Promised Land." Then Michael spread his mighty wings and flew out of the tent in a flash.

"We solved the first word!" said Peter. "One down and four to go."

They had just settled down on the soft mats on the desert floor to get a good night's sleep when Hank growled. His ears stood up, and he faced the door of the tent.

Mary sat straight up on her mat. "What's wrong, Hank?"

Peter crept to the tent entrance and peeked out. "Two guys are running out of the camp."

"Can you see who they are?" asked Mary.

"No," said Peter. "It's too dark."

"What do they look like?"

"They are wearing dark robes," said Peter. "One of them has a long beard and is carrying a bag under his arm."

"Maybe they're spies from Jericho," said Mary. "We need to tell Joshua."

"We don't have time." Peter peered into the darkness. "They're getting away! We have to follow them."

"I don't know—" said Mary.

Peter grabbed the adventure bag. "Trust me."

Mary took a deep breath. "Okay, let's go."

Peter took out the flashlight, and they headed

into the night to find the spies. They ducked as they ran between the tents.

Once they made it to the edge of camp, Peter pulled out binoculars. The moon was bright enough that he could see shapes in the darkness. "They're swimming across the river. It looks pretty rough."

He and Mary ran to the bank of the Jordan River. Peter looked at the rushing water.

"I'll go first," said Mary. "I'm a better swimmer."

"Okay," said Peter. He hated to admit it, but it was true.

Mary swam across the deep, swift water. "Come on, Hank!" she shouted.

Hank jumped in and made it across.

Then Peter waded into the rushing water. He struggled to hold the bag above water as he swam.

"Hurry!" said Mary. "What's taking you so long?"

Peter spit water out of his mouth. "I'm trying to keep the bag dry!" He swallowed another big mouthful and coughed. But he couldn't get a good breath. The wild water pulled him under. He kicked and twisted in the dark water. He was afraid he might have to let go of the adventure bag to save himself.

Then he felt Mary's hand grab him. He grabbed onto her with one hand, and with the other he gripped the bag. Together he and Mary fought the rough current and finally made it to the other side. Hank helped pull them out.

Peter lay down on the bank beside Hank, spit water out of his mouth, and took a deep breath. "Thanks for helping!"

"That's what family's for," said Mary, wringing out the hem of her shirt. "Is everything okay in the bag?"

Peter checked. The outside of the bag was soaked, but inside everything was dry. What a relief! "The scroll is safe," he said. "Time to get back to spying."

Peter, Mary, and Hank hid behind some trees beside the Jordan River.

Peter took out the binoculars and searched for the spies. "There they are!" he said. "They're running toward the city Joshua showed us."

"Jericho," said Mary.

Peter focused his binoculars. "There are towers along the wall with guards on top of them."

"Did the spies get in?" asked Mary.

Peter scanned the area around the walls. "I can't find them."

"Let me look," said Mary.

Peter handed the binoculars to Mary.

Hank shook water off. Peter wished he could shake water off his clothes.

"I don't see the spies either," said Mary. "I guess they went into the city."

"We need to get in there," said Peter.

Mary focused the binoculars. "I see the entrance. It has a big wooden and steel gate."

"Let's go!" said Peter.

"It's too late," said Mary. "The gate is shut. It's probably locked tight."

"I guess we'll have to wait until morning," said Peter. It would give their clothes time to dry anyway.

They hid in the bushes beside the Jordan River. Using Hank as a pillow, Peter and Mary soon drifted off to sleep.

MISSION JERICHO

The sound of birds singing in the trees woke Peter. It took a minute to remember where he was. Jericho! He sat up fast, pulled out the binoculars, and scanned the city walls. "The gate is open!" He poked Mary. "Get up! Let's go!"

Mary and Hank stood up. Peter dusted himself off while Mary washed her face in the river water. Then they headed to the city.

Peter stared up at the walls. "They're so high!"

The bottom part of the wall was made of big stones. The upper part was brick, and guards were standing on top. Peter pushed against the wall. "This is one solid wall," he said.

"It's one big fortress," said Mary.

Peter stayed in the shadows as he led Mary and Hank along the wall to the gate. Then they stood in a line of people entering Jericho.

"Uh-oh," said Mary. "I don't think we're blending in. People are giving us weird looks. And there's a guard!"

Hank gave a low growl.

"We have to stay calm," said Peter, although his insides felt jittery.

The guard checked the bag of the person in front of them.

Then it was their turn. Peter's heart pounded.

A man tapped the guard on the shoulder, and he turned.

Peter thought the man looked a lot like Michael the angel. "Hurry," whispered Peter. "Let's sneak

in." He held the
adventure bag tightly
under his arm as they
ran past the guard.

They ducked around
a corner. Hank panted.
Mary took a deep breath.
"That was close," she
said.

"Too close," said
Peter. "But we made it. Let's go find the two
spies we saw last night. We can look for the long
beard and bag." He led the way down a busy
street, trying to look like he belonged there.

They walked past house after house made of
brick and mud. But they didn't see the spies. They
searched through crowds of people buying and
selling, pushing and shoving. But they saw no
sign of the spies.

Peter picked up a jar in the market. "This looks just like the jar I knocked over at Great-Uncle Solomon's house."

"Yes," said Mary. "It has the same red and black zig-zags."

"Help!" A young girl shrieked. Peter looked around. No one seemed to care. People kept their heads down and continued shopping.

"Help!"

Peter put down the jar and frowned at Mary.

"What should we do?" said Mary.

"Help her," said Peter.

"We might blow our cover."

Peter looked around. "But no one is helping."

Peter wove through the crowd, trying to find where the cry for help was coming from. He looked back to make sure Mary and Hank were following.

Peter rounded a corner and found himself in a small alley. Three older boys stood around a little

girl. Peter thought she looked about five years old, and she was crying. The biggest boy grabbed a doll out of her hands and tossed it over her head to another bully. She jumped but couldn't catch it. The boys laughed at her.

"Doesn't look like a fair fight," said Peter.

The biggest boy turned and looked at Peter. "Looks like we have a hero," he said. "He looks a little wimpy in those funny clothes!"

The other bullies laughed and surrounded Peter. "What are you and your girlfriend going to do?" asked the biggest bully.

"She's my sister, not my girlfriend," said Peter.

"He needs his big sister to help him," said the second bully. They laughed and pointed at Peter.

Hank stepped in front of Peter and growled.

The boys backed up a little. One of them kicked sand on Mary.

"I wouldn't do that," said Peter.

The bully did it again.

Mary spun around and threw a karate kick in front of him.

Startled, he stumbled back and tripped.

"I told you," said Peter.

The other boys looked worried. The bully slowly straightened up and shook his fist at Mary.

Hank bared his teeth and growled louder.

"You better get out of here fast," said the bully. "And I better not see you around here again. Next time, I won't take it easy on you," he added.

Peter stood in front of the little girl and stared at the boys. They dropped the doll and left.

Mary handed the doll to the little girl.

She wiped the tears from her cheeks and hugged the doll. "Thank you."

"Do you know those boys?" said Mary.

"I think I recognized the biggest one," said the little girl. "I don't know the others."

"Why were they so mean to you?" asked Peter.

"They don't like my family." The little girl looked up and down the alley. "I have to go now. My big sister is waiting for me at her house."

"We'll walk with you to make sure you get there safely," said Peter.

The little girl led them through the streets to the city wall. She pointed up a stairway to a house built onto the side of the wall. "It's right up there," she said. "Thanks for helping me." She kissed Hank's head before she ran up the steps.

Peter, Mary, and Hank watched the girl open the door and skip into the house. Then they headed back into the center of the city to continue their search for the spies.

Peter spotted a noisy crowd. "Let's see what's going on," he said.

As they got closer, Peter saw that the crowd had gathered around a tall man in a black robe. "You don't need to be afraid of the Israelites!" shouted the man. "You are safe within these walls. You can defeat the Israelites."

Some in the crowd pumped their fists in the air and chanted, "Jericho will never fall!"

Others didn't seem as sure. One man shouted, "But the Israelites have defeated other kings!"

"Their God even parted the sea for them to walk across on dry ground!" called another man.

"Those stories are lies!" said the man in black. "The Israelites and their God are weak!"

Peter stepped forward. "That's not true!"

The man in black stopped talking and looked straight into Peter's eyes. Chills ran through him.

The man looked back at the crowd. "Don't be afraid," he said. "Trust your gods and your walls." Then he left, pushing his way through the crowd.

"I don't trust that guy," said Peter.

"Neither do I," said Mary. "There is something suspicious—and familiar—about him."

As Peter was trying to hear what the people were saying, he felt a hand grab his shoulder.

A Daring Escape

Peter turned to see the men he and Mary had been searching for. The one who had grabbed his shoulder had a long beard. The other looked younger and had a short beard. They both wore dark robes.

The older spy asked, "Aren't you the children Joshua found in the Tabernacle yesterday? What are you doing here?"

"We saw you sneaking out of the Israelite camp," said Mary. "We thought you might be Jericho spies."

"We are spies," said the younger man.

"I knew it," said Peter.

"But we are Israelite spies," he said. "Joshua sent us to spy on Jericho."

"My name is Caleb," said the older spy. "And this is Phinehas."

"I'm Peter, and this is my sister, Mary," said Peter.

"Woof!"

"Oh, yeah," said Peter. "And this is our dog, Hank."

"We're actually training to be spies," said Mary. "Can we help you?"

"I don't know. Maybe," said Caleb. "Just make sure no one sees you."

Peter cleared his throat. "Well, we might have a problem. I think the man in black saw us."

"Then we need to get you out of the city," said Caleb.

They ducked and darted through the crowded streets, heading for the city gate.

"There it is!" said Mary.

"Run for it," said Phinehas.

Peter froze in his tracks. "Wait!" he said. "The man in black is talking to the guards beside the gate."

Some of the guards drew their swords and stood by the gate. The rest of the guards left with the man in black.

"If he told the guards about you, they might be looking for us," said Caleb. "We need to find a place to hide."

They moved along the city wall looking for a safe place to hide. The sun started to set behind the tall walls.

Mary pointed to a stairway in the wall. "Look! It's the house where we took the little girl!"

"Let's go! Maybe we can hide there," said Peter.

They climbed the stairs. Peter knocked on the door.

A beautiful woman in a flowing red robe and gold earrings answered the door. Peter saw the little girl they had helped standing in the room behind her.

The little girl ran up and grabbed her sister's robe. "Rahab, these are the boy and girl who helped me."

Rahab leaned out and looked around. "Hurry! Everyone come inside!"

Peter glanced over his shoulder and thought he saw the man in black hiding in the shadows along the wall. But he blinked and the man was gone.

They hurried inside, and Rahab shut the door. She eyed Caleb and Phinehas. "Are you the Israelite spies everyone is looking for?"

"They are," said Mary.

"Word travels fast in this town," said Peter.

There was a knock at the door. Peter's heart pounded.

"Come with me," said Rahab. "I will keep you safe." She led them to a ladder in one corner of the room, and they followed her up to the roof.

The knock sounded again, harder.

"Quick!" whispered Rahab. "Hide under these stalks of flax."

Peter thought the flax looked a little like dry corn stalks. They all huddled close together and stayed very still as Rahab covered them. Peter hoped Hank wouldn't sneeze.

The knocking turned to pounding. Peter heard Rahab scurry down the ladder and open the door.

"The king of Jericho sent us!" said a gruff voice. "Bring us the spies!"

"I bet it's one of those soldiers from the gate," Peter whispered.

"Shh!" said Mary.

"Two men were here," said Rahab. "But I don't know where they came from."

"Where are they now?" shouted the soldier. It sounded like he was shoving furniture around and turning over chairs. Something crashed to the floor. The little girl began to cry.

Peter's heart pounded so loud that he was afraid the soldier would hear it.

"They're not here!" said Rahab. "They left Jericho when the gate was being closed."

"Where did they go?" asked the soldier.

"I don't know," said Rahab. "But if you hurry, you might catch them."

The door slammed and everything was quiet.

Peter and Hank were the first to crawl out of their hiding place. Peter took the binoculars out of his bag and looked over the wall, careful to hold them where the Israelite spies wouldn't see them. "The soldiers are leaving the city," he said. "They shut and locked the gate."

"Then we are safe for now," said Caleb.

Rahab poked her head through the opening in the roof. "They're gone."

Peter hid the binoculars in the bag as the spies crawled out of hiding. Mary brushed herself off. Hank sneezed and his whole body shook.

"Thank you for protecting us," said Caleb.

"I know that God is giving this land to the Israelites," said Rahab. "We have heard about all the amazing miracles your God has done to set you free from Egypt and protect you from kingdoms on the other side of the Jordan River."

Peter remembered all the amazing things he had seen God do.

"The people of Jericho are afraid," said Rahab, "because your God is the God of heaven above and earth below. Since I helped you, please promise that you will protect me, my parents, and my brothers and sisters when you conquer Jericho."

The spies looked at each other and nodded. "We promise our own lives as a guarantee for your family's safety," Caleb said. "If you don't tell anyone about us, we will keep our promise and protect your family."

"I won't tell," said Rahab. "Now we need to get you out of Jericho."

"How?" asked Peter. "The gate is closed."

Rahab pointed to a window.

Peter looked out and stared down the side of the high city wall. "I don't know—" he said. "That's a long drop."

Rahab pulled a long red rope out of a basket and tied it to a hook on the window. "Climb down this rope. Then go to the mountains and hide for three days until the soldiers return to Jericho."

The spies agreed.

"Leave this red rope hanging out of your window," said Caleb. "Everyone inside your house will be protected."

"Remember not to tell anyone about us," said Phinehas.

The spies grabbed the red rope and climbed out the window.

Peter watched as they lowered themselves safely down the outer wall to the ground. Then he

pointed to the red rope. "Ladies first."

Mary grabbed the rope and easily made it down the wall. Peter's hands started to sweat. He was a little afraid of heights.

"You can do it," said Rahab's little sister.

Peter slung the adventure bag over his shoulder. Then he took a deep breath, grabbed the rope in a tight grip, and slowly climbed down the wall. Halfway down, he panicked. "What about Hank?" he said, looking up to the window.

Rahab and Hank stuck their heads out the window. "Don't worry," said Rahab. "I have a plan."

A minute later, a basket dropped out the window. It was attached to another rope, and Hank was peering over the side. Peter and Hank reached the ground at the same time. Mary and the spies were waiting for them. Peter let go of the rope, and Hank jumped out of the basket.

Caleb pointed. "Let's get to those mountains!"

They all ran for the distant mountains under the cover of darkness.

Peter glanced back over his shoulder and saw a movement on top of the wall. He had a feeling that the man in black was watching.

Hiding in the Mountains

Peter, Mary, Hank, and the spies made it to the tall, dark mountains. They were steep and covered in sand and rocks, which made the climb difficult.

Mary stopped to take a breath. "There are no trees or bushes up here. Where will we hide?"

"There are caves along the top," said Caleb. "We can hide there."

They kept climbing and found two caves facing different directions on the mountaintop.

"You three stay in this larger cave," said Caleb. "We will stay in the smaller one."

"Keep watch over that side of the mountain," said Phinehas. "Let us know if you see the soldiers."

"We will," said Peter.

Peter, Mary, and Hank settled into the cave. It was big enough to walk around in. Peter took out one of the walkie-talkies and handed it to Mary. "I'll take the first lookout. You can rest." He told Hank to stay with Mary to protect her and the cave.

Peter walked a short distance and sat down on a big rock on the side of the mountain. He took the walkie-talkie out of his bag and pressed the red button. *Chhhh.*

"Come in, Monkey," he said. "The coast is clear."

Chhhh. "Okay," said Mary.

Chhhh. "Come in, Monkey," said Peter.

"What?" asked Mary.

"You are supposed to say over and out," said Peter.

"Fine," said Mary. "Over and out."

Peter could almost see her rolling her eyes. He looked through the binoculars for a while. He couldn't see much in the darkness, so he took out his journal and turned on his flashlight. He shielded the beam with his adventure bag, then he wrote.

Day 2

The stars are beautiful in the desert. You can see forever in the night sky. It reminds me of Creation and when we slept in the desert in Egypt. It's not easy being a spy. I hope I didn't mess everything up when the man in black saw me. I hope the soldiers don't find us.

Peter heard some rocks move, and he stopped writing. He heard footsteps behind him and turned, ready to run. But it was Michael.

"I will keep watch," said Michael. "You can go back to the cave and sleep."

"Thanks," said Peter. "For keeping us safe."

"Well, at least for tonight," said Michael. "Then I have to go and help lead God's angel army."

"What's going on?" asked Peter.

"Big things are about to happen," said Michael. "Go and get some sleep. You are going to need it."

Peter went back to the cave. With the adventure bag as his pillow, he fell asleep.

The hot sun crept into the cave and woke Peter. Hank was already sniffing around the cave, and Mary was sitting at the entrance. Peter stretched and joined Mary. The Israelite spies were coming around the side of the mountain.

"I'm so thirsty," said Phinehas.

Peter was thirsty, too, so he volunteered to get water from the stream halfway down the mountain. He left his bag in the cave but took the canteen and the walkie-talkie, which he hid in his pocket. It was a long way down the steep, rocky mountain, but it was easier than climbing up.

He finally made it to the stream. While he was filling the canteen, he heard voices in the distance. He ducked behind the nearest clump of bushes to hide. Then he pulled out the walkie-talkie and pressed the red button.

Chhhh. "Come in, Monkey," whispered Peter.

No response.

"Come in, Monkey," he said again.

"Shhh," said Mary. "I'm hiding so Caleb and Phinehas don't see the walkie-talkie."

"I might be in trouble down here," said Peter. "I need your eyes in the sky."

There was a pause. "What do you mean?" said Mary.

"Just look down here," said Peter. "Do you see anyone nearby?"

"Let me get the binoculars," said Mary.

There was another long pause. Peter heard more footsteps. He turned the volume lower.

Chhhh. "Come in, Bear," said Mary.

"What do you see?" whispered Peter.

"There are soldiers not too far from you," said Mary. "They're looking around. They might have heard something."

Peter felt the sweat pouring down his forehead. His heart pounded in his chest.

"They are walking toward the bushes," said Mary. "Don't move."

"*Grrrr.*"

Peter heard growling through the walkie-talkie. "Mary . . . I mean Monkey, are you growling?"

"No, it's Hank," said Mary. "He knows you're in trouble."

Peter looked up the mountain and saw Hank running down. He barked at the soldiers.

"Get that dog!" shouted a soldier.

They ran after Hank. He led them farther and farther away from Peter and the mountains.

Chhhh. "The coast is clear," said Mary.

Peter climbed the mountain as fast as he could. He tossed the canteen to Mary and grabbed the binoculars from her. He looked all around but couldn't see Hank.

"Hank!" shouted Peter. "Hank!"

"Shhh," said Mary. "The soldiers might hear."

"I don't care!" Peter whistled. He clapped his hands and called out—but Hank didn't come.

"What's wrong?" asked Caleb, coming up beside Peter.

Peter hid the binoculars behind his back. "Hank is missing. I have to find him!"

Keeping an eye out for the soldiers, Peter and Mary searched along the river. They crossed over the mountains. All day they looked for Hank, but couldn't find him. When it was too dark to search anymore, they headed back to the cave.

Peter tossed and turned. He was too worried to sleep. "God, please keep Hank safe," he prayed.

CROSSING THE JORDAN

Again, the morning sun woke Peter. He looked around the cave. Mary was still asleep, and Hank wasn't there.

Peter shook Mary. "Wake up. Hank's not back."

Mary stretched and sat up. Then she grabbed the binoculars. "Let's go."

They walked around the top of the desert mountain, looking in every direction.

"Hank!" shouted Peter.

Mary looked through the binoculars. "I don't see him anywhere."

At last they headed back to the cave. The Israelite spies walked up from the other direction.

"Did you find your dog?" asked Caleb.

Peter shook his head and sighed.

"He'll come back," said Phinehas.

"I hope so," said Peter.

They waited at the entrance to their cave and watched.

Peter licked his dry lips and grabbed the canteen. "I'm going down to get some water."

"Be careful," said Caleb.

As he bent down to fill the canteen, he heard something in the bushes. *Oh, no, not again.*

Peter got down and crept toward the bushes.

"Woof!"

Hank jumped out of the bushes. He knocked Peter over and licked him all over his face.

"Good boy!" said Peter. "You came back!"

Peter and Hank headed back up the mountain.

Mary ran to meet them and hugged Hank around the neck. "I missed you!" she said.

~◠~

After three days of hiding in the mountains, Peter, Mary, Hank, and the two spies started back toward the Israelite camp. Peter wasn't excited about having to swim across the Jordan River again, but Mary and the spies encouraged him. With Hank swimming alongside him, he made it. By the time they dried off, the sun was beginning to set. They all met with Joshua in his tent.

"God has given us the Promised Land," said Caleb. "The people of Jericho are afraid of us."

"Good work," said Joshua. He folded his arms and gazed out of the tent. "Tomorrow we leave for Jericho."

Peter, Mary, and Hank went back to their tent to get a good night's sleep. Peter was glad he didn't have to sleep on rocks again. He rubbed his neck and wrote in his journal.

Day 5

It was fun to work with the Israelite spies. It was exciting and dangerous—just like Great-Uncle Solomon said, but sometimes it was a little boring. Mary is reading the Top Secret Spy Training Guide in case we need to go back to work. We leave for Jericho in the morning. The spies gave us robes and sandals so we blend in better. I'm not sure how the little kids and animals are going to get across the Jordan River. I'm a great swimmer and I almost drowned.

~⁀⁔

When Peter looked outside the tent the next morning, he saw everyone busy packing their things. So he and Mary packed their tent, then joined the Israelites for a meeting.

Joshua stood on a rock. "Listen to what God told me." He pointed toward Jericho. "Today you will see that the living God is with you. We will finally enter the Promised Land."

Joshua turned to four priests holding something large between them on long poles over their shoulders. It was covered in a big blue cloth.

Mary nudged Peter. "I can see the shape of angel wings under the cloth. I think it's the Ark of the Covenant."

Joshua pointed to the priests. "Follow the Ark of the Covenant across the river."

"I was right!" said Mary.

"Why is it covered?" asked Peter.

Mary sighed and shook her head. "Only the Chief Priest is allowed to see the Ark of the Covenant. You should read your Bible more."

The priests carried the Ark toward the rushing river.

"I hope the Ark can float," said Peter.

As soon as the sandals of the priests touched the river, the water stopped flowing. It piled up into a wall of water in the distance.

The priests carried the Ark to the middle of the dry riverbed, and all the Israelites and animals safely crossed. Peter and Mary walked at the back of the long line of Israelites. Hank helped herd the sheep across.

Peter stopped and stared at the wall of water. He remembered how God had parted the Red Sea and helped the Israelites escape from Pharaoh and the Egyptians.

"Come on," said Mary. "Everyone is across the river except the priests with the Ark."

Mary and Peter ran to catch up.

When the priests carried the Ark out of the river, the wall of water crashed down and overflowed the banks of the river.

Peter grinned. "That was easier than swimming across."

"God always makes a way," said Mary.

The bag shook under Peter's arm. "We solved another word on the scroll!" said Peter. He pulled Mary behind a tree and took

out the scroll. The second word glowed and transformed into the word ALWAYS.

GOD ALWAYS

____ _____ _____.

"God always what?" asked Mary. "Always makes a way?"

No words glowed on the scroll.

"Always hears our prayers?" asked Peter.

Nothing happened.

"Those are all true, but that's not what the message is," said Mary.

Peter sighed and put the scroll back into the bag. "At least we have two words now. Three to go."

They ran back and joined the Israelites. As the sun set, Hank left the sheep and found Peter and Mary. They began to set up camp and prepare to enter the Promised Land.

Marching Orders

The next day, the Israelites prepared to go to Jericho. Peter watched the soldiers sharpen their swords and shine their armor. Then Peter and Mary helped the Israelites harvest grain from the fields. Hank helped keep the sheep from running away.

After a long day, Peter and Mary took a break in their tent. The first thing Mary did was take the scroll out of the bag.

Peter stared over her shoulder. "Have you solved it?"

"No," said Mary. "What if we don't solve the secret of the scroll in time?"

Peter got a sick feeling in his stomach. "I guess we'll be stuck here."

"We're halfway through our time, and we still have three words left," said Mary.

"I know," said Peter. "I can count."

Mary studied the scroll. "If we don't solve it, we'll never see Mom and Dad again." Her shoulders slumped.

"I miss them too," said Peter.

Hank laid his head in Mary's lap.

"We'll do it," said Peter, though he didn't know how.

"I hope so," said Mary.

Peter watched the bustling camp from the tent entrance. He looked over and saw Joshua leaving his own tent.

Peter turned to Mary. "Hey, Joshua is taking a walk. I wonder where he's going. Let's follow him."

Mary frowned. "We need to solve the scroll."

"Maybe if we follow Joshua, we'll find a clue," said Peter.

"Hmmm. You might be right," Mary said. "I'm stuck anyway." She put the scroll back into the bag and tossed it to Peter.

He caught it and said, "I guess we're back in the spy business."

Peter and Mary followed Joshua, staying back far enough that he couldn't see them. They trailed him out of the camp and across a rocky field.

"Where's he going?" whispered Peter.

"Is he headed to Jericho?" said Mary.

"He can't conquer Jericho alone," said Peter.

Mary squinted. "What's that in front of him?"

Peter looked through the binoculars. "Someone is standing in his path," he said. "And he has a sword."

"Who is it?" said Peter.

Peter adjusted the binoculars. "I can't tell. Joshua is in the way."

"Let's get a closer look," said Mary.

They crept closer and hid behind some bushes.

Joshua called out to the man with the sword. "Are you a friend or an enemy?"

"Neither," said the man. "I am the Commander of the Lord's Army!"

Through the branches, Peter could see Joshua bow. But he couldn't see the man who was talking.

"Take off your sandals," said the Commander.

"You are standing on holy ground!"

"What should we do?" said Mary.

"I guess we take off our shoes," said Peter.

They both quietly removed their shoes.

Then the big voice of God boomed, "I HAVE GIVEN JERICHO TO YOU. YOUR ARMY WILL MARCH AROUND THE CITY ONCE A DAY FOR THE NEXT SIX DAYS. SEVEN PRIESTS WITH SEVEN HORNS WILL MARCH IN FRONT OF THE ARK. ON THE SEVENTH DAY, MARCH AROUND THE CITY SEVEN TIMES."

"That's a lot of marching," said Peter.

"Shhh," said Mary. "Listen!"

"ON THE SEVENTH TIME AROUND JERICHO," said God, "THE PRIESTS WILL BLOW THE HORNS. WHEN THE PEOPLE HEAR THE HORNS BLAST, THEY WILL SHOUT WITH A GREAT SHOUT. THEN THE WALLS WILL FALL, AND THE PEOPLE WILL TAKE THE CITY."

Joshua put on his sandals and ran to camp.

Peter peeked through some branches to get a better look at the man who had been speaking with Joshua, but no one was there. So he slipped on his sandals. Mary was already heading out from behind the bushes.

Hank barked, and Peter looked up. Michael was flying toward them from the mountains.

As Michael landed in front of them, Mary asked, "Where have you been?"

"I have been preparing God's angel army for battle with Jericho." Michael pointed his sword to the mountains. Thousands of angels with shimmering swords were gathered there.

"Jericho doesn't stand a chance!" said Peter.

"I have to go and join the army," Michael said. "You only have seven days left to solve the secret of the scrolls."

"We're trying," said Mary. "It's not easy."

"Remember to be on the lookout for the enemy, Satan! He is working hard to stop God's people from entering the Promised Land." Michael spread his wings and flew away like a bolt of lightning.

Peter, Mary, and Hank walked back to the camp. The people were making the final preparations to enter the Promised Land. It was a night of celebration, song, and thanks to God. Peter wrote about it in his journal before going to sleep.

Day 7

Tonight everyone celebrated the Passover just like we did with Moses and his

family in Egypt. Everyone is so happy to finally be going to their new home. Oh, and I forgot to write about the manna. Every morning, God dropped it around the camp from the sky. We just went out in the morning and ate it. It's hard to describe. Manna is kind of like a cracker or a pita, but it tastes sweet like honey. Well, the manna wasn't there this morning. Instead we got to eat food from the Promised Land. It was very good. I am excited but a little nervous to go back to Jericho tomorrow. It's not a friendly place.

Peter put away his journal and tried to get a good night's sleep before the big day.

11

Around We Go

The next morning, the sound of a shofar blasted through the tent. It was so loud that Peter sat straight up. Hank howled.

Mary jumped off her mat with her arms up in a karate pose. "Are we under attack?"

Another shofar blasted. Then another.

Peter ran to the entrance of the tent and looked out. "No." He turned back to Mary. "The priests are just practicing."

Mary lowered her arms.

Peter peered back out and saw Joshua step out

of his tent. He wore a red robe with a leather belt holding a sword at his side. His helmet glistened in the morning sun. He held up his golden shofar and let out a long blast.

"Bring out the Ark of the Covenant!" Joshua shouted to the priests.

Everyone stepped back to make a path through the crowd as four priests dressed in white robes walked by carrying the Ark.

"Now, seven priests lead the way in front of the Ark!" commanded Joshua.

The priests marched in front of the Ark.

"Now, all the armed soldiers go to the front of the line!" shouted Joshua.

Peter stepped back as thousands of soldiers marched past with swords and shields.

When everyone was in position, Joshua said, "No one is to talk until the day I give the command to shout. Then shout like you've never shouted before! Now go forward! March around Jericho!"

The priests played their shofars as the people marched. Peter and Mary followed at the back of the line marching around Jericho. Hank trotted beside them. It was a difficult march over sand and rocks and hills.

As they passed the gate, Peter saw that it was locked tight. Soldiers lined the top of the tall wall, ready for battle. But a battle didn't come that day. They marched around Jericho one time, then marched back to camp. They did the same thing the next day. And the next. And the next. For five days, they marched around Jericho once a day and then returned to camp.

The days were long and hot and seemed to all run together. Some nights, Peter wrote in the adventure journal before going to bed.

Day 8

The march around Jericho was hard. The hot sun made me very thirsty. I'm glad that I brought the canteen in my bag. I could see the fear in the eyes of Jericho's soldiers standing on top of the wall. They looked confused when we marched away.

Day 10

My feet are starting to hurt from all the marching. Mary has blisters, but Hank doesn't get tired at all. He loves to go for walks. The Jericho soldiers don't seem as afraid anymore. They shout insults from the top of the wall. One of them said, "Look at the scared Israelites running away!" The Israelites didn't say anything. We just marched

away. I'd like to tell
those soldiers a thing
or two.

Day 12
Everyone is getting tired of marching.
Some are starting to complain and
wonder if Joshua knows what he's
doing. I heard one man say that he
wished Moses was still alive. It's hard
to wait for God.

As the sun rose on the sixth day of marching,
the shofar blasted and woke Peter. He stretched
his legs and rubbed his feet. He looked across
the tent and saw Mary studying the scroll.

"You're up early," said Peter.

Mary looked worried. "We only have two days
left to solve the scroll."

Peter lifted the flap at
the entrance of the tent
and watched Joshua
play his golden shofar.
"Why does he have to
play his shofar so loud
every morning?"

"The scroll is shaking!" said
Mary.

Peter looked over her shoulder as the
fourth word glowed and transformed into the
word HIS.

Mary read the scroll, "God always _____ his
_____."

"Defends his people?" asked Peter. But
nothing happened.

"Knows his plans?" guessed Mary. Nothing.

Peter heard the people gathering. He looked
out of the tent and saw the priests carrying the

Ark of the Covenant toward Jericho. "Time to march," he said.

Mary put the scroll back into the bag and handed the bag to Peter. Then along with Hank, they moved to the back of the line.

After marching halfway around Jericho, Mary said, "I'm tired of marching. Let's try to solve the scroll again."

As the Israelites marched ahead, Peter pulled out the scroll and unrolled it.

Mary stared at the scroll and scratched her head. "I've got it!" she said. "God always protects his people."

They waited, but nothing happened to the scroll.

"Good try," said Peter.

Mary looked up the wall. "It looks like we have company."

Peter looked up and saw the man in black

looking down. Peter rolled up the scroll and hid it in the bag. "I hope he didn't see it."

"I think he might have," said Mary.

They ran to catch up with the Israelites. Peter looked back, but the man in black was gone.

"Look," said Mary. "There's the red rope."

Peter saw it dangling from Rahab's window. "I wonder if she knows that the walls are falling tomorrow."

"We should tell her," said Mary.

"Rahab!" shouted Peter.

She didn't come to the window.

"What if Rahab and her family aren't in her house tomorrow?" said Peter.

"Then they won't be protected," said Mary.

"We need to warn her," said Peter. "But the city gate is locked."

"Maybe we can sneak in tonight," said Mary.

"How?" asked Peter.

"I have a plan," said Mary.

After finishing the daily march around Jericho, Peter, Mary, and Hank went back to their tent and prepared for their secret mission.

Mary read the *Top Secret Spy Training Manual*. "I have another idea," she said. "I'll be right back." She ran out of the tent. While she was gone, Peter tried to figure out the message on the scroll, but he couldn't solve it.

Mary dashed into the tent waving a scroll that looked just like their scroll.

"Where did you get that?" asked Peter.

"In the priest's library tent," said Mary. "The priest said I could have it." She buried the real scroll deep in the bag and put the fake scroll on top. "It's called a decoy."

"Why do we need a decoy?" said Peter.

"In case we get captured in the city," said Mary. "They might not find the real scroll."

"Good idea," said Peter. His palms started to sweat. "Do you think we'll be captured?"

"I hope not," said Mary.

They waited until the sun disappeared behind the hills. Then Peter led the way out of the camp, with Mary and Hank behind him. Under the cover of darkness, they made their way to the city gate.

"It's locked," whispered Peter. "How are we going to get in?"

"Do you have the lock pick that Great-Uncle Solomon put in the bag?" asked Mary.

Peter handed the pick to her and held the flashlight.

Mary started to work on the lock.

Peter looked around. "Hurry, before someone sees us!"

"This should do it," said Mary.

Click.

Peter pushed as hard as he could. The gate barely opened, but it was wide enough for them to squeeze through.

"It's too dark to look now. Let's hide until morning," said Peter.

They crept along the inside of the wall toward Rahab's house and found some big, empty baskets to hide in.

Peter told Mary and Hank goodnight. As he pulled his basket over him, he said, "I hope the man in black doesn't find us."

THE MAN IN BLACK

Peter woke again to the sound of a shofar coming from outside of the walls of Jericho. He peered out from under the basket he had slept in. Hank was already sniffing around the basket Mary was under. She lifted it up and yawned.

Peter rubbed the sleep out of his eyes. "The Israelites are marching early this morning."

"That's because they are marching around seven times today," said Mary.

"That means this is the last day of our adventure," said Peter.

"Unless we don't solve the secret of the scroll," said Mary. "Then we'll be stuck here."

"We have a lot to do today," said Peter. "Let's hurry and find Rahab so we can get out of here before the walls come down."

They crept out of hiding and dashed through the city, sticking to the shadows, ducking behind animals, and slipping around houses to keep from getting caught.

"All these houses look alike," said Mary. "How will we ever find Rahab?"

Then Hank barked and bounded up some stairs.

"Good boy." Peter ran up the stairs after him. "You found it."

Hank scratched on the door, and Peter knocked. But no one answered. Peter climbed another set of steps that led to the top of the wall. He looked over the wall and watched the Israelites marching past.

"They've made it around again," he said. "Where is Rahab?"

They searched up and down the streets in Rahab's neighborhood. They searched the well where women drew water. They searched the marketplace. In the public square in the middle of the city, they ran into a crowd.

Peter stood on his tiptoes and caught a glimpse of why the crowd had gathered. "It's the man in black," he said.

"Where?" asked Mary.

"In the middle of the crowd."

"Duck so he doesn't see you," said Mary.

Peter edged back behind a tall man.

"People of Jericho!" shouted the man in black. "You don't need to be afraid! Nothing is going to happen. It's just like every other day."

"Why are they walking around so many times today?" shouted an old lady.

"Yeah!" a man said. "They have already walked around four times."

"Maybe they need more exercise." The man in black laughed, and the crowd laughed along with him.

"Like I told you," said the man in black. "You can trust your gods and your walls to protect you."

Hank barked and pushed through the crowd. Peter and Mary squeezed through after him.

When they reached Hank, Rahab was standing next to him. "What are you doing here?" she asked. "It's not safe."

"We have a message for you," said Peter.

"Shhh," said Rahab. She looked around. "Come with me."

They followed Rahab around a corner and hid in an alley.

"What's the message?" asked Rahab.

"The walls are falling today," said Mary.

"When?" said Rahab.

"As soon as the Israelites march around seven times," said Peter.

"Then we better hurry and find my family," said Rahab.

She led Peter and Mary around the city, searching for her family. They found her parents in the marketplace.

Rahab ran to them. "It's time!" she said. "Find the rest of the family and meet at my house."

"Oh, my!" said Rahab's mom. She put down her groceries and hurried away with Rahab's father to look for the rest of the family.

Peter, Mary, and Hank stayed with Rahab and searched for her brothers and little sister but couldn't find them.

"We're running out of time," said Mary. "We have to get to your house."

"Maybe your parents found them," said Peter.

They headed back to Rahab's house. They climbed the stairs, went inside, and shut the door.

Rahab quickly counted everyone in the house. "Oh, no!" she cried. "My little sister is missing!"

"You stay here," said Peter. "We'll find her."

Rahab picked up her little sister's doll. "What if you can't?"

Hank walked over and sniffed the doll.

Mary said, "God will help us."

Peter ran out of the house and down the stairs. "Let's go," he called to Mary and Hank.

"Where could she be?" said Mary.

A lady on the street shouted to a man on top of the wall, "Are they still marching?"

"They've gone around six times!" he answered.

Peter's heart pounded. "We better hurry."

Hank sniffed the air and took off running.

When Peter and Mary caught up with Hank, Rahab's little sister was petting him.

"Your family is waiting for you," said Mary. "Come with us."

They ran back toward Rahab's house and began climbing the stairs up to the door. They were halfway up when, suddenly, someone grabbed Peter's bag from behind and pulled it off his shoulder.

Peter turned. It was the man in black!

"Where do you kids think you're going?" said the man in black.

Mary stepped down beside Peter and threw a karate kick right in the middle of the man's chest.

He tumbled down the stairs holding Peter's bag.

Peter turned to Rahab's sister. "Run to the house!"

The little girl ran up the stairs and pounded on the door. Rahab opened it and grabbed her little sister in her arms.

"Go inside and lock the door!" shouted Peter. "This might get ugly."

The door slammed, and Peter heard the lock turn. He turned and looked down the stairs.

The man in black slowly began to climb the stairs again. "Nice karate kick. I think that's what you call it." His grin was not friendly.

"How do you know about karate?" said Mary.

"We've met before," he said. "A long, long time ago. You might recognize me."

Peter didn't remember meeting him. But there was something very familiar about him—and the sinister look in his eyes.

"Were you in disguise?" asked Mary.

"Maybe," said the man in black.

"Are you a spy?" asked Peter.

"Sometimes," said the man in black.

"What's your secret code name?" said Mary.

"I have many names," said the man, "but you probably know me as The Snake."

Hank growled.

"We should have known it was you, Satan!" said Peter.

Satan climbed a few more steps. "It looks like you're all alone. Michael must be busy."

"We're not alone," said Mary. "God is with us."

Satan looked around. "I don't see God. It's just us."

Peter ran up to the top of the wall and pointed over it. "Don't forget the Israelites."

Satan shoved past Mary and Hank and joined Peter at the top. Peter felt a chill and edged away.

Satan sneered. "The Israelites are pitiful and weak. They will never take this city."

"Yes, they will," said Mary. "Haven't you learned anything about God's promises?"

The scroll shook inside the bag Satan was holding. He opened the bag and pulled out a scroll. "Let's see what powerful secrets are inside this scroll."

MISSION ACCOMPLISHED

Peter's heart pounded as Satan unrolled the scroll.

Satan squinted and held it up to the sun. "There's nothing on here. It's blank!"

"Maybe you just can't see the truth," said Peter.

"There is no truth!" Satan ripped up the scroll and threw it over the wall.

"Give me back my bag!" said Peter.

"So you want your bag?" said Satan. He held it over the side of the wall. "Well, too bad!" He dropped it over the side.

"No!" Peter shouted as he watched the bag drop to the ground.

"Michael! Help!" Mary called.

A ball of light blazed through the air to the bottom of the outer wall. Michael picked up the bag and flew to the top of the wall. "I think someone dropped this," he said.

"Well, if it isn't Michael flying in to save the day," said Satan. He lunged for the bag.

Michael blocked him with a shield and handed the bag to Peter. Then he pulled out his flaming sword. "Not today, Satan."

The shofars blasted from outside the wall.

Peter looked over and saw Joshua holding his golden shofar.

"Shout, for the Lord has given you the city!" commanded Joshua.

All the Israelites shouted. The sound grew louder and louder.

Satan looked over the wall. "What's all the shouting about?"

"You're about to find out!" said Peter. "Because God always keeps his promises."

The bag shook in Peter's hands, and the wall shook under his feet. Then the wall cracked and shifted.

Mary ran up the rumbling stairs, jumping from one step to another as the stairs began to crumble.

"Grab my hand!" shouted Peter.

Mary reached for Peter and jumped as more steps fell away.

Peter grabbed her hand and pulled her to the top of the shaking wall.

"Ruff! Ruff!"

Peter looked down and saw Hank at the bottom of the crumbling stairs. The bag continued to shake in his hands. "Hank, come!" shouted Peter.

Hank ran up the remaining steps and stopped where the stairs had fallen.

Mary clapped her hands. "Come on, Hank! You can do it!"

Hank leaped over the missing stairs, right into Mary's arms.

"You can't trust God!" cried Satan. "The Israelites will never get the Promised Land."

Peter reached deep into the bag and pulled out the real scroll. They had figured out the message. Without even looking, Peter knew what the scroll said. "God always keeps his promises!" he said.

The scroll shook again. Peter unrolled it, and the last words glowed, transforming into the exact message he had guessed: GOD ALWAYS KEEPS HIS PROMISES.

Satan stumbled along the top of the shaking wall. "You're not getting away this time," he growled.

PROMISES

The walls kept shaking and shifting and cracking. The big chunk of wall where Satan was standing fell right out from under him, and he tumbled to the ground.

Peter held the scroll tight. Mary clung to Hank. The walls crumbled beneath them, and they fell too. Peter squeezed his eyes shut, ready to hit the pile of rubble below.

He gasped as he hit something soft. When he opened his eyes, he saw that he and Mary and Hank had landed on the big, fluffy couch in Great-Uncle Solomon's library. Peter was still gripping the scroll.

Hank leaped out of Mary's arms and shook himself.

Mary brushed dust and crumbled wall out of her hair. "That was too close!"

"Way too close," said Peter. He stood up, wiping off dust and rubble.

The scroll's red wax seal transformed into a golden medallion and fell to the floor. Peter picked it up and looked at the inscription of the Ark of the Covenant.

Great-Uncle Solomon rushed into the library and came to a stop. "It looks like you had an amazing adventure."

Peter told Great-Uncle Solomon about the Israelite spies and about Joshua and crossing the Jordan River. He told about the tall walls of Jericho and about Mary using the spy tools to unlock the gate.

"You two have become quite the spies," said Great-Uncle Solomon.

"Woof!"

"And you too, Hank," he said.

"I hope Rahab and her family were okay," said Mary.

Great-Uncle Solomon went to one of the shelves in the library and pulled out his big red Bible. "Let me tell you the rest of the story."

He told them about how Joshua led the Israelites to conquer the Promised Land. He told them that Israel trusted God, and there was peace in the land—for a time. "Not only was Rahab okay," he said. "She lived with the Israelites and was the great-great-grandmother of Israel's greatest king."

"Who?" asked Peter.

Great-Uncle Solomon put his Bible back on the shelf. "That is a story for another day."

"You promised to tell us what artifact you found when you were a spy," said Mary.

"I almost forgot," said Great-Uncle Solomon. "Follow me."

He took them down the hall and up the stairs to a room they hadn't been in before. Inside on a shelf was a long wooden box. Great-Uncle Solomon opened it and pulled out a golden shofar.

"That's Joshua's golden shofar!" said Mary.

Great-Uncle Solomon beamed. "I knew it!"

"Knew what?" asked Mary.

"This shofar was found at an archeology dig at Jericho," said Great-Uncle Solomon. "It proves that Joshua and the Israelites conquered Jericho just like the Bible said."

Peter looked at the Ark on the golden medallion. "Did you ever find the Ark of the Covenant?"

Great-Uncle Solomon shook his head. "No, not yet. Maybe someday."

"Maybe we can help," said Peter.

Great-Uncle Solomon smiled. "Maybe you will. But for now, you have more adventures to come."

Do you want to read more about the events in this story?

The people, places, and events in *Journey to Jericho* are drawn from the stories in the Bible. You can read more about them in the following passages of the Bible.

Joshua chapter 1 tells the story of God asking Joshua to lead the Israelites into the Promised Land.

Joshua chapter 2 tells the story of the spies and Rahab.

Joshua chapter 3 describes how God parted the Jordan River.

Joshua chapters 4–5 tell about the Israelites preparing to enter the Promised Land.

Joshua chapter 6 tells the story of the wall of Jericho falling down.

Numbers chapter 13 tells the story of when Joshua was a spy.

CATCH ALL
PETER AND MARY'S ADVENTURES!

In *The Beginning*, Peter, Mary, and Hank witness the Creation of the earth while battling a sneaky snake.

In *Race to the Ark*, the trio must rush to help Noah finish the ark before the coming flood.

In *The Great Escape*, Peter, Mary, and Hank journey to Egypt and see the devastation of the plagues.

In *Journey to Jericho*, the trio lands in Jericho as the Israelites prepare to enter the Promised Land.

In *The Shepherd's Stone*, Peter, Mary, and Hank accompany David as he prepares to fight Goliath.

In *The Lion's Roar*, the trio arrive in Babylon and uncover a plot to get Daniel thrown in the lions' den.

In *The King Is Born*, Peter, Mary, and Hank visit Bethlehem at the time of Jesus' birth.

In *Miracles by the Sea*, the trio meets Jesus and the disciples and witnesses amazing miracles.

In *The Final Scroll*, Peter, Mary, and Hank travel back to Jerusalem and witness Jesus' crucifixion and resurrection.

ABOUT THE AUTHOR

 Mike Thomas grew up in Florida playing sports and riding his bike to the library and the arcade. He graduated from Liberty University, where he earned a bachelor's degree in Bible Studies.

When his son Peter was nine years old, Mike went searching for books that would teach Peter about the Bible in a fun and imaginative way. Finding none, he decided to write his own series. In The Secret of the Hidden Scrolls, Mike combines biblical accuracy with adventure, imagination, and characters who are dear to his heart. The main characters are named after Mike's son Peter, his niece Mary, and his dog, Hank.

Mike Thomas lives in Tennessee with his wife, Lori; two sons, Payton and Peter; and Hank.

For more information about the author and the series, visit www.secretofthehiddenscrolls.com.